My Friend Lucky

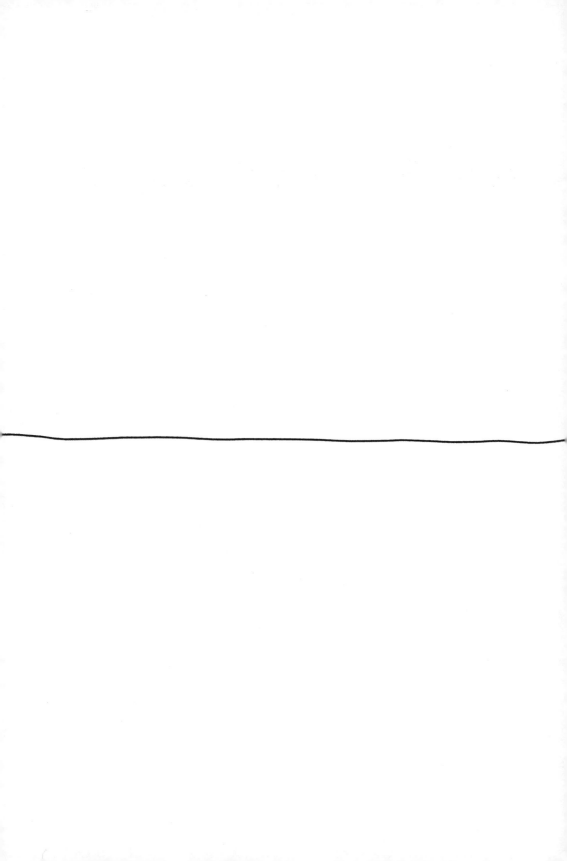

My Friend Lucky

David Milgrim

Ready-to-Read

Simon Spotlight

New York   London   Toronto   Sydney   New Delhi

SIMON SPOTLIGHT
An imprint of Simon & Schuster Children's Publishing Division
1230 Avenue of the Americas, New York, New York 10020
This Simon Spotlight edition May 2017
Copyright © 2002 by David Milgrim
For information about special discounts for bulk purchases, please contact
Simon & Schuster Special Sales at 1-866-506-1949 or
business@simonandschuster.com.
Manufactured in the United States of America 0417 LAK
2 4 6 8 10 9 7 5 3 1
Library of Congress Cataloging-in-Publication Data
Names: Milgrim, David, author, illustrator.
Title: My friend Lucky / David Milgrim.
Description: New York : Simon Spotlight, 2017. | Series: Ready-to-read. Level 1
| Summary: A dog named Lucky demonstrates opposites such as slow and fast,
dry and wet, cold and warm, and here and there.
Identifiers: LCCN 2016031407 (print) | LCCN 2016041029 (eBook) | ISBN
9781481489027 (hardcover : alk. paper) | ISBN 9781481489010 (pbk. : alk.
paper) | ISBN 9781481489034 (eBook)
Subjects: | CYAC: English language—Synonyms and antonyms—Fiction. |
Dogs—Fiction.
Classification: LCC PZ7.M59485 My 2017 (print) | LCC PZ7.M59485 (eBook) |
DDC [E]—dc23
LC record available at https://lccn.loc.gov/2016031407

for wyatt
with all my heart

Lucky gives.

Lucky gets.

Lucky's here.

Lucky's there.

Lucky's hungry.

Lucky's full.

Lucky's sad.

Lucky's happy.

Lucky's big.

Lucky's small.

Lucky's slow.

Lucky's fast.

Lucky's dry.

Lucky's wet.

Lucky's loud.

Lucky's quiet.

Lucky's cold.

Lucky's warm.

Lucky's lost.

Lucky's found.

Lucky chases.

Lucky's chased.

I love Lucky.

Lucky loves me.